Priscilla McDoodleNut DoodleMcMae ASKS, "Why?"

Written by
Janet Mary Sinke

Illustrated by
Craig Pennington

My Grandma and Me Publishers

Dedicated to all those who dare to ask, "Why?"

"The beauty of the night depends upon the unique reflection of every star."

-Janet Mary Sinke-

On a moon spinning 'round

in a place far away,

Lived . . .

Priscilla McDoodleNutDoodleMcMae,

A girl who was common, considered quite shy,
Till one day she questioned two kings with a "Why?"

Now . . .

King Norman would order his servants each day
To fashion his hair in a very strange way.

They curled it and piled it on top of his head.
And Norman, he thought, since his hair was all red,

That he, in some way, was above all the rest.
He said, "I've been chosen to lead a great quest,

To rule over all with my gorgeous, red hair
While sitting up high on my red, ruby chair."

"WHAT!" cried the voice of another smug king. "Why, I am King Wynthor. I know everything.

I'm good and I'm kind. People call me a saint.
I've ruled through the years without any complaint.

And as you can see, yes, my hair is all blue.
That makes me much smarter than someone like you!

So listen. Don't question. Do all that I say
And that includes Norman. He too must obey!"

And they argued for hours. They argued all night.
They argued who's wiser. They argued who's right.

They pounded the table. They stomped on the floor.
They made such a racket then argued some more.

But those who were present . . . they heard not a word
For they were all sleeping. Not one of them stirred

Except for Priscilla and Wynthor's baboon
Who feared for all people who lived on their moon.

Then . . .

Both kings in their anger drew lines in the sand,
Two lines that divided not only the land,
But also the hearts and the minds of those there
Whose heads were all covered with red or blue hair.

And just when it seemed things could not get much worse,
Both kings called a meeting. King Norman spoke first.

"Beginning today," the old king cleared his throat,
"I'm here to enforce a new law that I wrote,

A law that forbids any person," he said,
"To speak their own mind if their hair isn't red.
For since we are kinder, much nicer than you,
Your voice will not count if your hair is all blue."

Well . . .

The blue-haired moon people upon hearing this
Stood up and they screamed and they shook a tight fist,
And made funny faces while scrunching their noses
At all those whose hair looked like red-colored roses.

Wynthor, he sneered at old Norman and said,
"Your brain . . . it's all jumbled inside of your head.
'Tis I who will lead. I am King. I decree
That every moon person must answer to me."

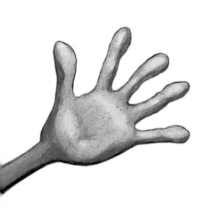

And tensions, they grew in each face on the moon,
Including the face of one, hairy baboon.
His whole body trembled. He felt his heart race
'Cause people were screaming all over the place.

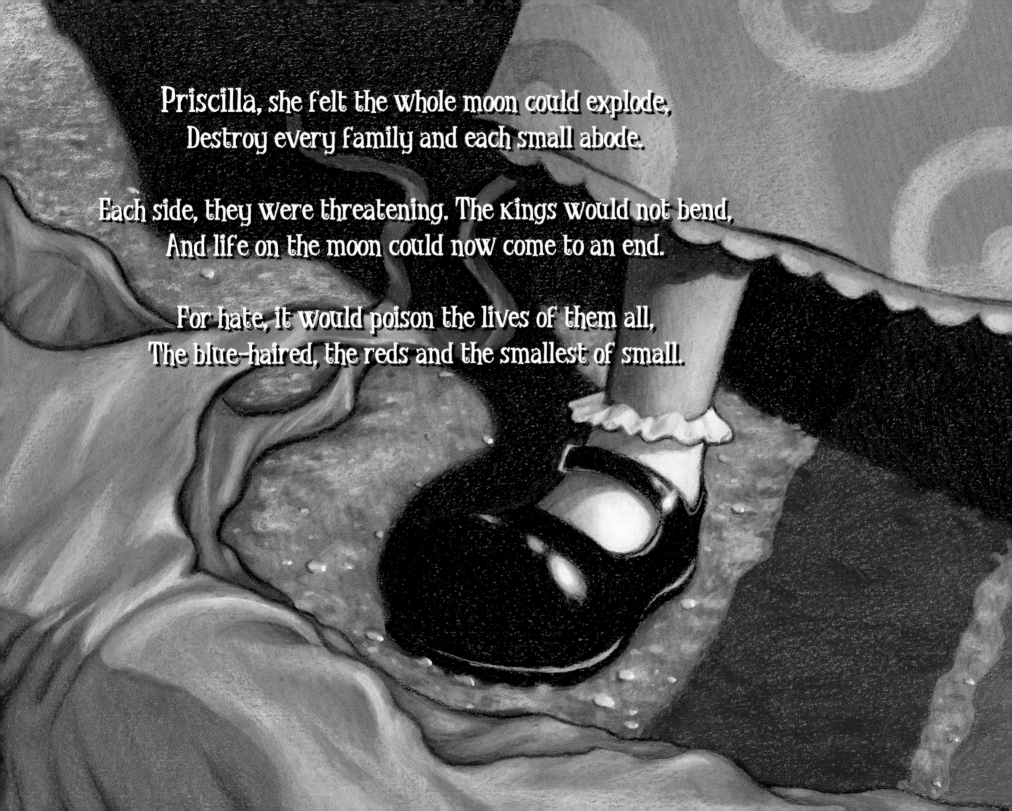

Priscilla, she felt the whole moon could explode,
Destroy every family and each small abode.

Each side, they were threatening. The kings would not bend,
And life on the moon could now come to an end.

For hate, it would poison the lives of them all,
The blue-haired, the reds and the smallest of small.

So . . .

Priscilla stepped out from the loud, angry crowd.
She inched her way forward. She nodded, then bowed.

And then with great courage, she did something fine,
So fine and so brave, she stepped over each line.

Then slowly she reached. She uncovered her hair.
And everyone gasped at the girl in the square,

For there stood Priscilla, the curls on her head . . .

Were stunning deep PURPLE
Not blue or rose-red.

The crowd, they stood frozen. What would the kings say
To young Miss McDoodleNutDoodleMcMae?
She was, after all, just a shy little kid.
And no one much cared what a little kid did.
But . . . Priscilla was different. She stood in the square.
Now searching for courage to speak for those there,

And though just a kid, she was sure of one thing:
The moment had come to now challenge each king.
She shook. She heard Norman. He bellowed, "Come here!
You've broken my law, and my law is quite clear.
No purple-haired person can live on this moon.
So pack up your bags. You must leave by twelve noon."

Then Wynthor, so saintly, went down on one knee.
He sneered back at Norman. He said, "I agree.
This girl, she must go. I don't like her at all.
She's strange, and she's different. She's weak, and she's small.
And so I command that she leave here at once.
She may not return . . . not for ten thousand months."

Priscilla stood firm in the warm summer sand
While longing for someone to hold her small hand.
She needed a friend, and she needed one now,
And then he came forward. He gave a small bow.
One scared, brave baboon, he would tempt the moon's fate.
He leaned, then he whispered . . .

"The Purple Looks Great!"

And those four simple words from that simple baboon
Gave strength to Priscilla to speak for the moon.

"Your majesties, please," she looked up to the sky,
"I have just one question. My question is **Why?**"
"Why," asked Priscilla, "do eyes fail to see
The good that is present in you and in me?

For though we are different we still are the same.
We cry and we laugh and we each have a name.

And all these good people, the red and the blue,
Should have the same rights as your majesties do
Including the freedom to live without fear
At peace with our neighbors and those we hold dear."

The crowd had unfrozen. She'd spoken quite plain
With words that now clicked in each moon person's brain.
"Why," they now questioned, "was purple hair wrong,
And **Why** shouldn't all colors of hair get along?"

Why, they now thought, can't we live side by side,
Together in peace with no lines that divide?
And **Why** can't this moon be a home for us all,
No matter what color, no matter how small?

And while they stood thinking, both kings from their thrones
Now studied Priscilla with moans and with groans.
They had no real answer. She asked them again.
But this time the question was louder and then,

A strange thing, it happened, the red and the blue
Now asked the same question and that's when she knew,
Their moon could be saved if they only would try
And so with one voice they together asked, **"Why?"**

And their Why was so strong and so loud and so clear
That it shook the small moon. There was panic and fear.
The shaking it spun them, it twirled them around,
And they got all mixed up as they fell to the ground.

And next, it so happened, that red and blue line,
It split from the shaking. It seemed like a sign
That life might get better. Each stretched out a hand
To help one another stand tall in the sand.

And since that great day, most who live on this moon,
Including one special, brave, smiling baboon,
Have learned in their homes, in their cities and schools
To live and uphold these important moon rules:

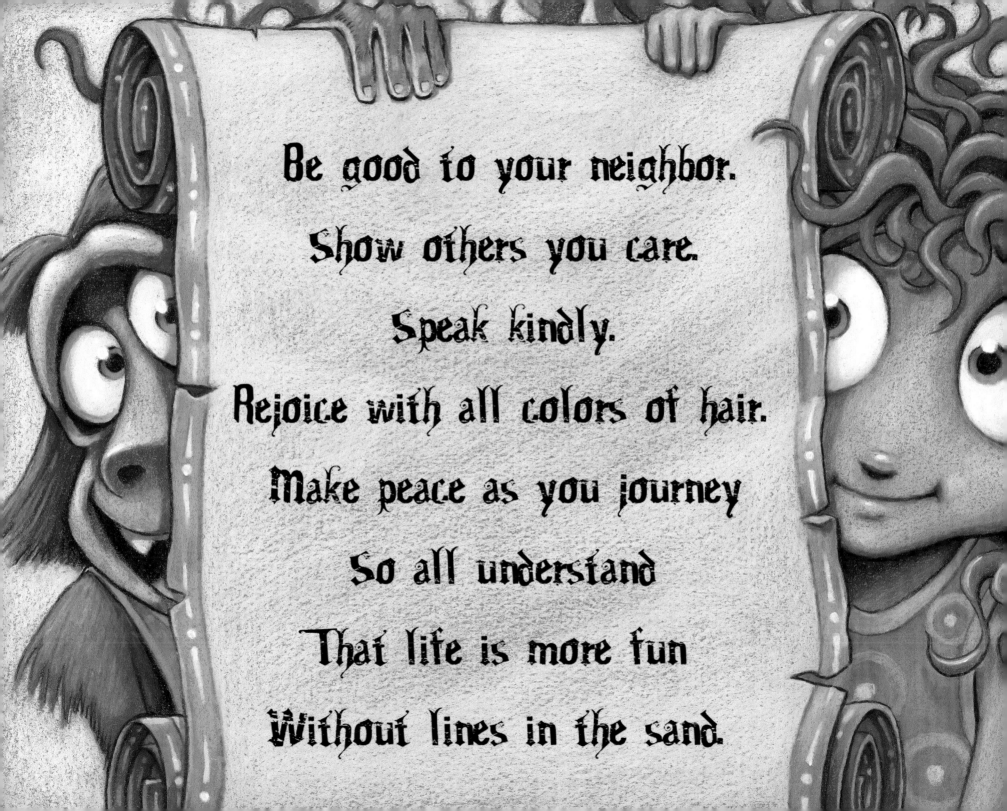

So simple these rules, they now echo in places
Where others with different but charming new faces

Now travel on moonbeams or sometimes a star.
And tails of fast comets bring those who live far.

For glimmering out in the dark of the night
Are joyful new rays from a peaceful new light,

A light that now welcomes all colors of hair
With arms that are open and willing to share.

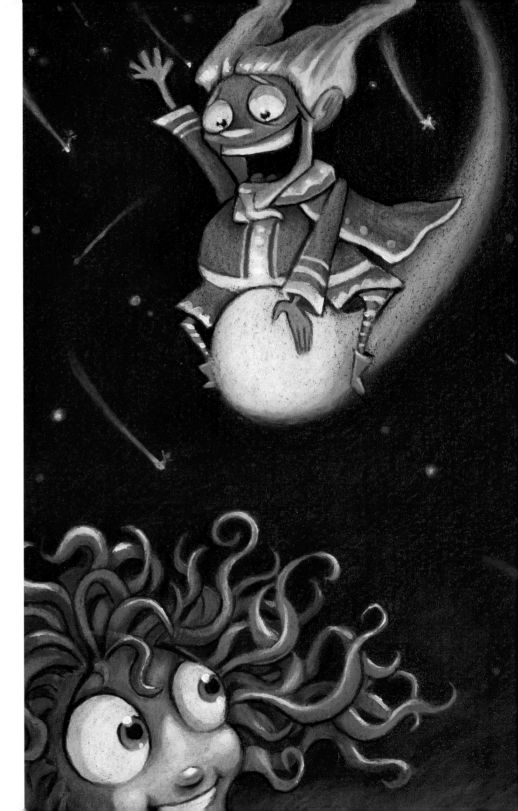

And Norman and Wynthor now sit all alone
Up high on a hill with no servants or throne.
They still don't quite get it. They choose not to see
The good that is present in you and in me.

A rather sad thing when you think it all through.
Two stubborn old kings who have nothing to do

Except to just sit and complain, "It's not fair,
That one little kid with her strange-looking hair,
Considered by most to be common, quite shy,
Could make such a difference with one simple **Why?**"

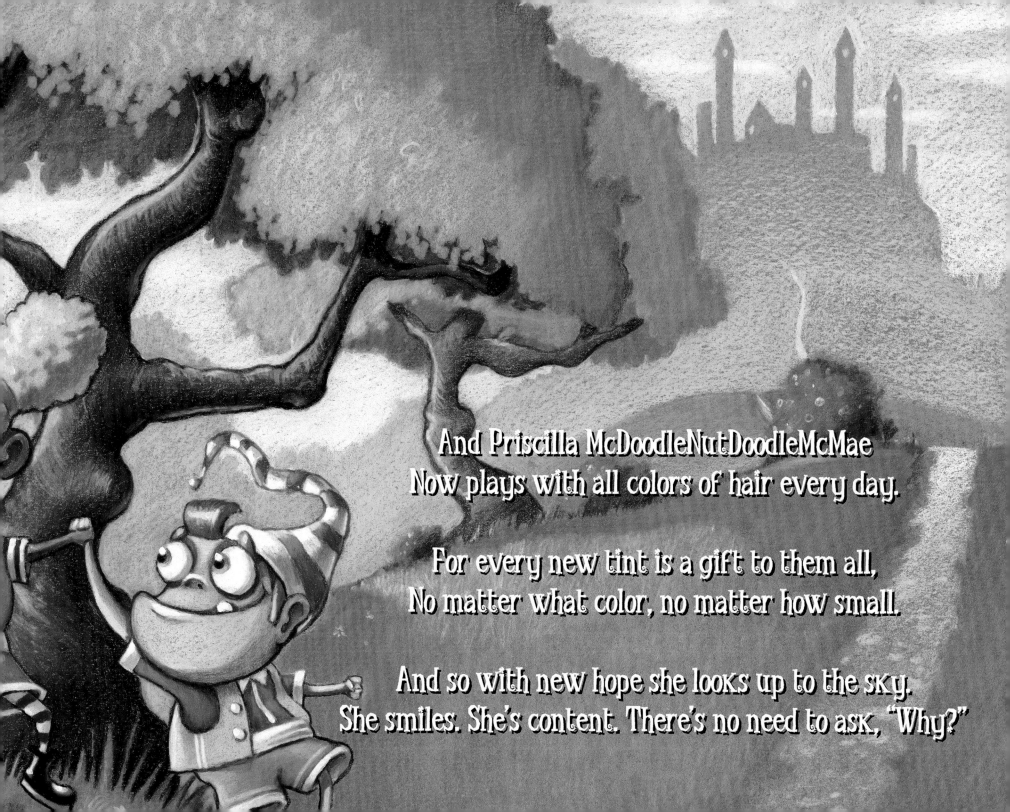

And Priscilla McDoodleNutDoodleMcMae
Now plays with all colors of hair every day.

For every new tint is a gift to them all,
No matter what color, no matter how small.

And so with new hope she looks up to the sky.
She smiles. She's content. There's no need to ask, "Why?"

THE ~~END~~ START OF A
BRAND NEW BEGINNING

First Edition
Printed and bound in Canada

Janet Mary Sinke
My Grandma and Me Publishers®
P.O. Box 144
St. Johns, Michigan 48879
989/224-4078
Website: www.mygrandmaandme.com
E-mail: info@mygrandmaandme.com

ISBN-10: 0-9742732-8-7
ISBN-13: 978-0-9742732-8-0
LCCN: 2007901430